Welcome Baby

VIOLET

Stick your favorite picture here

A special message for you

Welcome Baby Violet, welcome to the world,
Amazing things for you will unfurl.

A wonderful journey awaits you ahead,
Life will guide you where you need to be led.

VIOLET

Each day for you will be an adventure,
Explore the colors, the smells, and the textures.

All birds and animals welcome you too,
To support and encourage in all that you do.

Welcome Baby Violet, your birth was divine,
Good things await you, your life will be fine.

Great places call you, there's so much to see,
Look down at the world from high up in a tree.

The mountains, rivers, forests, and seas,
Want you to visit whenever you please.

You will meet lots of people,
they'll all be your friends,
All around the world, in different lands.

You'll experience the weather,
and how things all change,
The heat and the cold, the sun and the rain.

And with the weather, comes all the seasons
You'll love them all for so many reasons.

The winter has snow,
and summer's light showers,
In autumn leaves fall,
and in spring the plants flower.

Welcome Baby Violet,
the whole world welcomes you.
It's exciting to see everything that you'll do.

You'll visit the cities and the countryside,
Where you want to live you'll get to decide.

Every where's beautiful,
every where's a delight,
Whether in the daytime or even more so at night.

VIOLET

These wonders are waiting to greet your eyes,
The earth, and the oceans, the starry night skies.

I'm sure all you see, and all that you learn,
Will bring you great joy, and knowledge, in turn.

Everywhere you go,
you'll discover new treasures,
They are there for a purpose,
to give you many pleasures.

So, welcome Baby Violet, do not waste a day
This world is your toy box. It invites you to play.

67476629R00024